Be <u>praised</u>, O God,
in all your creatures!

Jack Wintz ofm

St. Francis
in
San Francisco

by Jack Wintz, O.F.M.

Illustrations by Kathy Baron

Paulist Press
New York/Mahwah, N.J.

Caseside illustration by Kathy Baron
Caseside and book design by Saija Autrand, Faces Type & Design

Library of Congress Cataloging-in-Publication Data

Wintz, Jack.
    St. Francis in San Francisco / by Jack Wintz ; illustrations by Kathy Baron.
      p. cm.
    Summary: A young boy and his dog join St. Francis on a tour of the city of San
Francisco.
    ISBN 0-8091-6684-4
    1. Francis, of Assisi, Saint, 1182-1226—Juvenile fiction.   [1. Francis, of Assisi, Saint,
1182-1226—Fiction.   2. San Francisco (Calif.)—Fiction.]   I. Baron, Kathy, ill.   II. Title.

PZ7.W76835 St 2000
[E]—dc21

                                                                                    00-050117

Published by Paulist Press
997 Macarthur Boulevard
Mahwah, New Jersey 07430

www.paulistpress.com

Printed and bound in Mexico

Praise to the happy star
that shines over the sacred place
where God entered the family of creation!

Author's Dedication
For Josh, Noah, Thomas, Cyrus, Lincoln, Oliver, Thea Viola, Erin, Sarah, Caleb, Jessica, and Stella.   *J.W.*

Illustrator's Dedication
Dedicated to Reinhold, my support and inspiration, and also to Chris and Greg, who kept up with the housework so that I could paint! Thank you!   *K.B.*

Hi! I'm Sunpatch, the Thompsons' dog. My golden hair shines like a patch of sunlight. At least, that's what the Thompsons say—and that's how I got my name.

One sunny October afternoon, Johnny Thompson and I were running along a path in Golden Gate Park in San Francisco.

I stopped at a small lake to lap up some cold water. Suddenly, my ears flipped straight up. A strange voice was calling me!

"Brother Sunpatch! Oh Brother Sunpatch!"

I turned around and saw a friendly little man. He had fur on his face just like me and was wearing a raggedy brown robe with a white cord tied around it. *Who is this little fellow?* I wondered.

Johnny walked right up to him and blurted out: "I know all about you! You're St. Francis of Assisi. Your statue's on the birdbath in our backyard. You're the saint who loves animals—and you're the patron saint of San Francisco!"

"Johnny's right, I am St. Francis," the man said to me. He held my paw in his warm hands. "I'm happy to meet you, Brother Sunpatch."

"Why are you here?" Johnny asked.

"Today is October fourth, my feast day," St. Francis replied.
"It's a perfect day to visit San Francisco, the city named after me.
I've come to this park first to meet the animals who live here."

St. Francis cupped his hands around his mouth and
called out at the top of his voice:

"Hello, all you creatures of the park! Come over here, please. I have a treat for you!"

From every corner, animals began running toward St. Francis and gathered at his feet: rabbits, squirrels, birds, raccoons—even a buffalo from the buffalo pen.

The saint laid his hands on the animals and blessed them. "My brothers and sisters of the woods and fields and lakes," he said softly, "we are all creatures of one family. We are all brothers and sisters.

"What do you think about that, Sunpatch?" he asked, rubbing my floppy ears. "You and I have the same Father in heaven. Doesn't that make us brothers—members of the same family?"

Francis then walked over to a tree filled with birds. Smiling, he told them: "My dear sister and brother birds—always praise and thank your loving Creator. You have been given feathers and wings. You fly freely through the air—over housetops and lakes. You sing cheerful songs and find food without having to work for a living. How God must love you!"

Brother Francis sat on a tree stump next to us and said, "Sunpatch, Johnny, and all you other animals, you are all very lovable and good. You have been created by a God of overflowing goodness.

"Even more, this same loving God entered the family of creation two thousand years ago. The Most High God was born among us as a human child named Jesus. By making his home in our created world, God gave great value to all creatures everywhere."

"That's why I have brought treats for you," said St. Francis, pulling from his sack a healthy handful of peanuts, raisins, sunflower seeds, and other grains. My goodness! There were even dog biscuits for *me*!

"Now I have a special favor to ask of you," St. Francis said to Johnny and me. "I've always wanted to ride the famous cable cars of San Francisco. Will you join me on this adventure?"

Johnny nodded yes, while I wagged my tail until it felt loose.

We hurried down a side street and hailed a taxi.

Recognizing St. Francis in his tattered brown robe, the cabbie said with a chuckle, "If you are who I think you are, I'd be honored to drive you around at no cost, for as long as you wish! And that goes for the little kid and dog, too!"

"Thank you, my good sir. We want to go downtown and ride the cable car. But before that, I hope you can take us on a short side trip to Mission Dolores."

As we hopped in, Johnny asked Brother Francis,
"What is Mission Dolores? And why are we going there?"

"Mission Dolores is another name for Mission St. Francis, or *San Francisco*
in Spanish. This little Spanish mission church on Dolores Street is the
birthplace of the city of San Francisco."

"The mission was founded in 1776 by my followers, Franciscan friars from Spain. It was one of twenty-one Franciscan missions founded along the California coast when this land belonged to Spain."

Inside the mission, St. Francis led us to the small
chapel. He knelt down on the floor near the altar. Johnny
knelt on his left, while I sat as still as a statue on his right.

"Most loving God," our friend said with great reverence, "I pray, first of all,
for the American Indians who lived here when my Spanish followers arrived in
California more than two hundred years ago. Bless them all. I also ask your
blessing upon all the people in San Francisco today, and all the animals, too."

After visiting the rest of the old mission, we returned to our taxi.

"Now, Brother Taxi Driver," said St. Francis with a grand gesture, "let's be off to the cable cars!"

"At your service!" the driver laughed with a smart salute, and we hurried off toward downtown San Francisco.

Clang! Clang! Clang! we heard as we approached Powell and Market Streets, where the cable cars leave for Fisherman's Wharf.

"I'll be waiting for you at the end of the line," our cabbie offered, as the three of us rushed to the cable car.

Fearing that pets would not be allowed aboard,
I glanced at the conductor.

He winked at me and said, "I can't refuse you a seat,
pup, seeing that you're a friend of our city's patron saint!
Sit here at the front window."

With that, the cable car began to jog along the tracks. The car
was packed with a great mix of people—young and old, black, white,
brown, and yellow—some from far-away lands like India and Japan
and the Philippines.

Joking with the cable car operator, St. Francis and Johnny laughed and smiled and enjoyed themselves as the cable car climbed toward the summit of Nob Hill.

"This is wonderful! What a hoot!" St. Francis shouted to the operator. "Here we are, brothers and sisters from all over the world taking a happy ride together. Even Sunpatch is with us to represent the animals. The whole family of creation is here having fun. This is the way the journey of life is meant to be!"

"Right on!" the operator shouted back, ringing the bell.
"Woof! Woof! Woof!" I echoed, and the car exploded with laughter.

The cable car rattled along the edge of Chinatown, turned left onto Jackson Street, right onto Hyde Street, and then climbed the biggest hill of all toward Lombard Street. I pressed my nose against the front window, but was afraid to look.

When the car reached the summit, I opened my eyes. What a sight! Far below lay the blue waters of San Francisco Bay, and off to the left stretched the glorious Golden Gate Bridge.

"What a wonderful city!" exclaimed St. Francis. "So full of beauty and charm and breathtaking sights!"

"Yes, the perfect city to be named after you," the cable car operator replied. "The whole world knows you as the happiest of saints—the one who never stops praising God for the beauties of creation."

When we reached the bottom of the hill and the end of our ride, our cabbie was waiting. "Hey! St. Francis, Johnny, and Sunpatch! I'm over here," he shouted as we thanked the conductor and the operator and climbed off the car.

"It's getting late, Brother Driver," said St. Francis. "We need to return to Golden Gate Park so Johnny and Sunpatch can get home in plenty of time for supper."

Driving past the crowds milling about Fisherman's Wharf, the taxi driver headed back toward Golden Gate Park. On the way, St. Francis thanked us for sharing our afternoon with him.

"I hope you remember my message to you and to the animals in the park," our favorite saint said to Johnny and me. "We are all brothers and sisters in the sight of our loving Creator, and we owe each other great love and respect."

Back at the park, Brother Francis stepped out of the taxi and gave Johnny and me a warm hug. With his hands over his heart, he said, "Brother Sunpatch and Johnny, I will never forget you, or this day, or this beautiful city!"

Our sadness quickly turned to joy as we watched St. Francis stroll into the park, praising God for the trees and the animals, for the birds and the lakes, for Johnny and me, and for all the people in San Francisco. Oh yes—and for cable cars, too!